Alphabet of Love Serial

1/26/16 — for Barbara,
in wonder at your work,
which I've not really
seen yet!

Jon

Alphabet of Love Serial

LOU ROWAN

REALITY STREET

Published by
REALITY STREET
63 All Saints Street, Hastings, East Sussex TN34 3BN,
UK
www.realitystreet.co.uk

First edition 2015
Copyright © Lou Rowan 2015. All rights reserved.
Cover & author photos by Andrea Augé
Typesetting & design by Ken Edwards

A catalogue record for this book is available from the
British Library

ISBN: 978-1-874400-67-7

for Jed Myers

Prelude

My body tingles and my eyes water. Bows scraping, mouths wetting reeds, fingers toughened by bass-strings—it's physical. But I am wearing a suit, my collar is tight. The players wear black dresses, suits. Don't their clothes restrain them from doing what they drive me to feel?

Music is a dog that changes when you move to the country. It explores your property, makes it his with strategic sprays. It barks at squirrels birds and butterflies, and digs up rodent holes. It disappears for hours that worry you if you notice, for you've moved out there to do your work at last. There's a new tone to its barking and growling: deeper from the chest, higher out of control, bugling and screeching that give your friends pause when they arrive.

And the blood—where did the blood on its mouth and shoulders come from? You worry it's been wounded, but you can find no scratches or holes on a body whose hair seems coarser and which suffers your touch without affectionate preening.

But your work engrosses you, and you pay less attention to the dog than you did in the city when you needed attention and affection focused on you because you felt abused by your job your family or by your self, when you were so needy the licking the hot breath the 60-pound body launching its needs at you satisfied like a huge sticky cinnamon roll.

It plunged its nose under the tails of your friends' dogs when they visited from the city, distracting your visitors from their compliments to your tasteful new place as you kissed them noisily on both cheeks, their pets curling up and cringing in corners to protect their vents.

When Custer was obliterated Brahms took friends to dinner to celebrate the Indians.

The woodwinds combined with brass and strings in what my music appreciation teacher called thick harmony, his lips moist, the tympani booming, surge at me, and I wonder for the 459th time whether I'm correct to allow music access to my nervous system, whether it is in fact an abstract evolution of mathematical interrelations, a game the composer and the musicians play while the uninitiated like me pant over them ignorant as a dog.

If you could lie down in the auditorium as you now can on certain large airplanes, if you could make love to your partner instead of contenting yourself with holding her hand on her thigh or your thigh, if the bed could be by huge windows giving on the bay, if you could cease to distract yourself by wondering if your partner wants to hold your hand, likes your clothing, or wishes you were dressed like the thinner man in the better seats three rows down to the left, and if your bladder would stay empty despite the tea you drank to sharpen your senses—maybe you could be a music whose moist tingling you could discharge ecstatically between her thighs.

The lassitude that had absorbed released and banished my parents' inhibitions of me, a parousia more engulfing than my dog's ecstasy wriggling on his back,

8

or a killer's triumph bagging his prey, the blood surging through me maximally oxygenated, words, words that shoot from my past to perforate my presence released, gone, and I would be music, music, music.

A exhales; B moves closer. In a room heated to 70°, a body at 99° radiates heat to 22". The pulse and respiration of bodies within this mini-climate accelerate 1.37 times faster than bodies beyond. A's resting pulse (reclining reading self-help materials before she dressed for this occasion) of 65 rises to 85. As A's respiration speeds from 12 to 20, the fluctuations of her upper body create proportionate effects on B's rates.

Other propellants to A and B's hearts and lungs: their beverages—stimulant, sedative, neutral? The oxygen and carbon dioxide levels of the social air. The volume of conversation and music shocking A's systems but stimulating B's.

And B's words induce A to flush and perspire. Has her heightened respiration and circulation mimicked exercise? Does her physical condition—for she combines aerobic and anaerobic exercise 6+ hours weekly—moderate her reactions? Why do we work to improve our health if not to improve our lives?

A complains she "freezes" at social gatherings, absorbing proximity, volumes, timbres too efficiently for her own good—defined as the ability to specify which among her reactions will guide her.

We may never know what B said to A in those 13 minutes, their buttocks perched on the back of a settee occupied by the host and the hostess, whose backs leant away 4" away from them.

Seconds into the 14th minute, A suffered her right bicep to be grasped by B, who steered her towards the bathroom.

17 of the 21 persons in the room could adduce circumstantial evidence that B preferred women over all alternative sexual objects.

As they neared the bathroom, B applied her palm to A's bare neck, and pushed her into the small room by thrusting her forearm between A's scapulae. She closed the door, stepped between A and the mirror, and dropped her heavy purse next the hot water spout. Her face 6" from A's, so that A could smell astringent wine and something more organic scenting her breaths, she dabbed away the green mascara beneath A's eyes with a gentleness A could remember no parent nurse doctor or lover applying to her flesh. A's breathing ceased and her pulse raced as B murmured, "There! Now, we can see those lovely eyes!"

Sitting or standing, moving or taking a stance. There are 21 in the room, and 15 know each other by name. The music, something technical from Europe, is loud and the walls are bare save for the iconic Newman whose edges are imperceptible, wall and canvas the same pale ivory, and the black vertical line could be a wire, could be leading to a speaker producing the sounds, perceptible after 10 minutes, that aggregate and feed back the conversations in the room, phrases scrambled but words and sources distinguishable, issuing from 7 speakers and 2 subwoofers, and the sounds of glasses, of chairs moving, of heels on abstract parquetry, of doors, and of dishes on the glass tables scrambled into an interval-system that supplies rhythm to the voices, a metronomic rhythm, a pulse-interval the system of whose governing program might be recognized critically this new century.

The 15 known names are of 2 through 15 syllables combining given and family names, and there are 3 with foreign prefixes, 1 honorific. The 6 unknown names sit, stand, move, or take stances. The correlation of the music to these motions could be measured. Correlating the utterances of the 21 to these measurements could be essayed provisionally and discretely, for instance:

As D, a known, released himself from 3-minutes with his former spouse and business partner, he inhaled and exhaled deeply 2 feet from C, an unknown, who had taken a stand near the drinks table, but whom the music had stimulated to move without conscious objective, but he was aimed at the same 5 squares of parquetry to which the exhaling D was turning from his encounter with the too-well-known, and the awkwardness of their near-collision caused them to chuckle and look into each other's green eyes and moderately-anxious faces while lightly restraining each other with fingers to shoulders, allowing the fingers to trail down and linger on bicep and forearm, as each uttered, unsynchronized, a "Well hello," caught by the music and diffused throughout the huge room while C and D took stances face to face in their space.

The clothesrack was 20" long, and E's size was towards the large, long extreme. E waited for noontime shoppers to leave, shuffled about the store, forcing his attention onto object after object, none registering in his memory, so that when he addressed them a second time and a third time, they remained novel and alien. Cufflinks, wrist chains, belts, wallets, ties, shirts, socks, collar stays, sweaters, jackets, tasseled loafers, he studied them all without the help of sales clerks, and without purpose until he judged the area around his intended rack clear.

The sounds dotting the large space dizzied E, the wisps of conversation between fathers and sons, between raucous teens, between tailor and buyer before a mirror, the strains of the live piano music from the stairwell by the music student who made E feel guilty because she was ignored by the crowds, her sonatas tempting him to stand over the piano and hope she appreciated his love of music and his wish that he could make her feel better, followed by his chiding himself that she probably was accustomed to the neglect, that she could have picked pieces by Eric Satie intended for these circumstances, and guilt that he was looking at her beauty, wondering if he'd have the same feelings were it a young man, then remembering that last week when he approached the same rack too soon for the seasonal change it *had* been a young man and he had experienced the same sequence of effusions and confusions he could never tell his wife; and so now he felt only more befuddled as he approached the rack, hoping the pleats were finally gone at the large long end, for he was not to wear bulky pleats, no matter what size his girth.

E's weight varied ± 20%, his embarrassment proportioned to its magnitude. When he sat his belt constrained his belly, so he wore XXL shirts, sweaters, jackets to mitigate the bulging overhang. His senses dulled, his social skills declined as the bulge grew. His erectile function weakened, and he apologized to anyone concerned, including sometimes himself. Pleats left his loins ill-defined, which he sensed was exactly what they were. He did not believe D.H. Lawrence when he wrote "loins," but he believed that most other men—and he cast his eyes about the store and saw copious examples—were happy with their loins and their functionality. When his penis was soft and withdrawn, like a baby's, he could not believe that it was a valid, competent penis, something for which women could long. He felt women as a demand he must avoid, like the clothsrack. He was relieved when his wife allowed him to shop alone. He loved the term "wallflower," and longed to find one, his own, maybe (he told himself as he made his final circle) that was why his love-experiences were so confusing: they were substandard, and clarity could exist only in standard love-experiences, and if he could only bring himself to do something about his appearance, he could do something about his loins and his love.

He could not avoid women, because he felt inadequate alone, and inadequate felt worse than incompetent, and because alone was eccentric—and though he was capable of being eccentric, he was not capable of suffering the judgment of others that he was eccentric. He might have tried to play the piano, had he been more willing to be eccentric. He was bitter at all the failed loves in his life: he was as angry with them as he was with the clothesrack, now coming towards him and in focus, and there, even more annoying, a tall young man was pulling a pair of unpleated trousers from precisely the spot E had targeted and retargeted. He said "fuck it"—under his breath he thought—and the young man, last week's piano player, turned and smiled: "Yes, I hate shopping too."

In hospitals the relationship between the machines, the instruments, the labyrinth of corridors, the rushing gowned bodies, the smells suggesting chemicals and secretions, and the human perceptual apparatus is exploratory at best. The unreason of hospitals is constant through history. To be a patient tests free will as radically as a family of origin.

G repeatedly passed out in medical circumstances. When he was young and drinking he saw a black-and-white movie, "The Brink of Life", and he couldn't withstand the threat of the birthing ward, smelling the hospital in the Greenwich Village theatre, and left hastily to pass out by the curb on Bleecker Street. He passed out twice more in Village hospitals, once during day surgery to remove a ganglion bulging from his back, and once while his vas deferens was cut loose. He passed out as a teenager near Wilshire Boulevard when his oral surgeon showed him the incision, red like his imagination of a vagina, from which his wisdom teeth were being taken.

When he was admitted to the same Greenwich Village hospital for an intestinal illness he was in pain and feverish. Access to his infection was through his sphincter, and preliminary information about its extent and nature was obtained manually. He sat for 2 hours in an examination room, to be joined not by his specialist but by 7 interns and residents, for St.

Vincent's is a teaching hospital. Face down on a gurney, he was probed by each of the 7 as they discussed his infection, leaving their fingers in there as they talked. His anger and his pain prevented his fainting, but because he was unsure what lay ahead in this hospital he did not remove his anus from their fingers, even when they asked him questions implying that passage was a location of his sex life.

His specialist elected conservative treatment, which sounded reassuring to G. G visualized his intestine as a soft hose with a hole in it, surgery would tape or reattach the ends of the hose, after which he would have a new set of pains to deal with, and a new set of explanations to present his visitors. His roommate in the semi-private suite was Hiram, an old man undergoing consistent attention from nurses and residents, requiring Hiram's bed to be curtained from G's. A nurse chuckled over Hiram, who was cantankerous and old, her chuckle implying he had a right to be. Hiram was an improvement over Dave, who'd moved on to the cancer floor. Dave discussed endlessly his longing for Ray's Original Pizza, right around the corner, but forbidden to him. When Dave's wife visited, she said, "Now Dave, you know you can't have it." To which he would reply, "But it's *Ray's Original Pizza.*"

G felt bad about himself; he had a non-fatal and somewhat vague illness. G didn't know how to respond to Dave's cancer, but he noticed that Dave was apologetic too, apologetic to the doctors and nurses because he did not understand what they were about to do to him. Dave never asked why, he tried, haltingly, to grasp what.

Dave disappeared while G was exercising in the hall: 50 L-shaped laps pushing his IV post.

Hiram stared at G when his curtain was open, but did not respond when G greeted him politely. His skin was grey where his beard sprouted and pale ivory elsewhere, his legs and arms smooth like prosthetic devices.

G's continual objective was to make adjustments to his life that would make him feel good about himself: if he felt good physically, and even looked good, he would feel good generally. This hospital stay was progress towards the objective because he was not eating; conservative treatment dictated he give his bowels a rest, and his visitors marveled at his figure but derided his experimental mustache.

Talking with patients along the hall, G concluded that they saw themselves, sheepishly, as defective products, and his heart might have gone out to them did they not disappear, and did not he struggle not to believe everything inside him that wanted to agree with the hospital's treatment of him and them.

He longed for visits from his specialist, and for signs that his intestines were being treated. His worst moments were trivial: when he could not hold in the enema as long as the nurse demanded and rained from his bowels too soon; when he was kept waiting in an empty hall beyond the sonogram center for 2 hours, sitting on his sore spot in a wheelchair the orderly did not bother to brake, letting it glide towards the fire door until its rail bumped the dirty yellow wall and G, who had forgotten his book, facing the wall.

He longed to be walking, competent, jaunty like the doctor who showed him his sonogram of the bulge pressing his bladder. "Mr. G, you're not pregnant are you!" she exclaimed and he forced himself to laugh, but could find no riposte.

G's relief from his bodily and his general malaise was television and sleep. He began to find visits from friends oppressive, for they brought him back from stupor. He awoke at 2:00 AM to Hiram's voice. "Oh, Mama, MAMA." He awoke at 4:00AM, partially conscious of sounds of curtains, gurneys, bodies moving near him.

The nurse who couldn't exonerate G for his failed enema told G, "Oh him, he died."

For the rest of his stay G had the suite to himself. The pain in his intestine remained, but his temperature lowered, the internal symptoms, according to his specialist, ameliorated. Surgery would not be required. G felt forgiven by the hospital, but as he thought about his exoneration he realized that the hospital wouldn't have done it, it had to be something else.

I

I's bedroom was down the hall from his mother's; he slept with his younger sister, who was behind a screen, a demarcation I honored carefully. I remembers the screen, remembers the blackboard easel on which he taught himself to write. His teachers were women; he longed to please them. He shaped letters with slavish perfection at the blackboard, was thrilled to have a few square feet of the classroom in his bedroom. The capital "I" was, Mrs. T said, like a spoon at the bottom: you began, careful always to work one continuous stroke, by making a reverse small "l" but you DIDN'T STOP you CONTINUED, "THAT'S RIGHT I! DON'T STOP!" right through the bottom of the spoon up about a quarter or third of the "l" and the PAUSE at the tip of the crescent like the moon on its side, children, and now STRAIGHT BACK ACROSS the board to the bottom of the l-loop, and "look how well I is doing it, I want you all to do it just like I."

I's sexual fantasies were purposeful. He brought girls from his classroom to join girls from the neighborhood, mostly friends of his sister, into his enlarged bed, and he taught them. Authoritative, he taught them how to pee properly, which normally required him to demonstrate the strength of his stream. His heart went out to the girls, the impulse to teach them humming through him. He taught them to overcome the mistakes that came so naturally to girls, putting their clothes on when they should be off, for example, or paying attention to each others' silliness when their whole beings should be fastened on an I transfixed by his calling to teach them.

I remembers his mother singing in the kitchen, her voice so lovely he thought she was the radio, and she chuckled when he told her that. He was struggling in the patio with his assignment from his stepfather to tie a bowline knot. He succeeded after weeks of tearful frustration when he found an illustrated knot-book, and the little arrows in the diagram taught him the way that in his stepfather's fast-moving or even slow-moving hands eluded him.

He forgave ugly girls in his fantasies. A girl on his schoolbus named Becky worked at the cannery. He brought her to bed and held her scaly red hands, forcing her to give them up to him, filling her with strength to acknowledge them. Masterful, he disciplined his disgust for her fishy smell, her rough flesh, her harsh name.

I remembers the hallway separating his bedroom from the living room and the kitchen. He knows it led to his mother's bedroom, but he cannot remember her end of the hall, or the bedroom. He remembers noxious smells from his mother's bathroom, but not the bathroom.

I remembers dinner: the table set neatly, the butter-dish and the huge beaded glass of whole milk flanking the silverware, the chafing-dishes of vegetables, potatoes, pastas, boats of sauces, gravies all waiting, like I and his sister, for the adults to arrive, and then to seat themselves properly, lifting the chairs carefully across the thick shag rug, so as not to jerk them, as I had, into the table and spill the tall glasses.

If there was soup, the extra spoon to be dipped away from I's body but delicately tipped towards his lips, a little insuck of air to pull it in, but it is not to be blown on. The salad-fork was smaller than the main-course fork, and salad was easier to take in, required fewer corrections or directions from I's mother than soup, but it was boring compared to what he wanted: the meats she served, especially hamburger tastefully enhanced with fragments of bread and onion, ham sweetly glazed, roast beef in plate-size slices. The tiny salt-spoon dropped the salt in clumps I tried furtively to spread across the juicy surface. Artichokes were fun because of the melted butter and because you could use your fingers, more fun than bread because the butter must be spread so thin you couldn't taste it, or because the butter-pat was unsalted.

I tended to lose concentration, and would be caught picking at his vegetables, sawing them with his fork-tines, rather than taking the trouble to pick up his properly-angled knife, or caught racing through the meat, causing him to be "full" in the middle of the vegetables.

B was his sister's friend, her father a doctor. B was a hero at this table because she was of such exemplary politeness: she finished everything served her (though she was small and thin unlike I and his sister), politely accepting seconds, but even more because on two occasions she excused herself to hasten to the bathroom through the kitchen to throw up. When I had boils, B's father lanced them, and instructed him on bringing their pus to the surface with hot compresses. I can still find the scars on his legs, shoulders, and wrist from the boils.

Seconds were a painful decision for I: balancing his

shifting perceptions of what his mother wanted against what was happening inside his shirt and trousers.

Dessert was sweet but often too complex, too adult. I's ideal sweets were brownies, which his mother made so rich you could stand the walnuts, Hershey bars without nuts, or frozen Snickers bars. Eskimo pies were good until I ate near the wood stick.

Stewed fruit was a frustrating dessert, warm but not sweet enough. Apple and cherry pie were tart, but a la mode they were perfect: huge, and satisfying to stupefaction.

Dessert took less time than the early courses, and while working at it I knew that, once he had carefully cleaned his plate, done everything he possibly could within his skill-set to clear the table and tidy up , he could sink into relative relaxation on the sofa before the TV, and during commercials he would be allowed into the icebox for more dessert, should he rinse his dish properly, and he knew that his mother's attention would be directed towards the screen, not towards him and his sister. And maybe it would be Lucy or Gracie, and he could giggle unchecked.

J

Athletics were awkward, except tetherball. Tetherball was simple: you struck the ball squarely with the inside of your fist; you hit it hard down, so that it would rebound from its nadir at your feet and leap at and over your opponent. The trajectory was like those rings around Saturn that were never level in the photos in Life Magazine. Then you timed the ball's return from over your opponent's head, stepping out of its way to slug it down—maybe twice more as the rope shortened. Now you could soften the angle and the blows as the rope climbed the pole, until soon you were jumping to tap it as its radius tightened, its speed increased, the opponent's helplessness engulfing him or her. Three easy things: slug it down, time its return for a follow-up slug, tap it to keep it speeding to the kill at an angle flatter to the ground.

J got them. He rarely lost at tetherball, and confirmed his talent 30 years later when he played his then-therapist at a summer camp his children and the therapist's enjoyed at Woodstock, and his slugs and the therapist's hapless responses were predictable if disconcerting.

J's mastery extended partway into tennis: he could hit hard serves. He thought he was hitting a hard topspin serve like his father's, but a tennis lesson 40 years later showed him he was hitting flat. He could throw a baseball hard, and skip rocks effectively. But 29 years after his intramural pitching career, he tried to show his sons how to throw a curveball at their summer camp, tore his rotator cuff or something else with a complex name in his shoulder, and has been sore ever since. That tear reminded him that when he pitched his curveball at his high school rival it went in flat as a board, and his screwball failed to move. So he wonders whether he really could bend the ball, or whether his sinker and his screwball were fantasies, though he remembers an ump, his music teacher, marveling over his curve's drop.

He wrestled in high school because it required such extreme effort, so much discipline. It is unclear to this day whether he enjoyed wrestling, even though he turned around his losing record bigtime as a senior and qualified for a tournament. His arms were long, and he made up for his lack of strength and defined muscle with strategy and leverage. His stamina was average.

There's a yearbook picture of him in agony. He was in stalemate, trying to throw a switch his opponent, visible only as hindquarters, is countering, and he is grimacing as if someone were crucifying him or squeezing his testicles. He does not remember feeling that bad.

Were his expressions, like his curveball, exaggerations? Is there in athletics a proper way to hold the face? What is the relation between exertion and mood? How do one's physical limitations define one's moral and mortal limitations? Is there a sport at which J could have excelled, had he found it and persisted in it? Would he be a better or happier man?

J began to jog before he withdrew from mood-altering substances. He was a physical wreck from age 20, when his using curtailed his exertions, until age 36, when he began to read the literature of redemption by running he marked and inwardly digested. He learned that healthy runners set themselves goals, and he set himself the goal of running around the Frederick Law Olmsted park in his borough. His early runs were out-and-back along the flat segment of the 5-sided park, his goal a traffic circle where gay men and pot smokers gathered. He joked about collapsing into their clutches. When his flat segments numbered the equivalent of a run around the park he tried to, but failed because it was a hot day and because the park's remoter segments were hilly. But he persisted through his first success on a cool day. And this he accomplished before he was clean, and he persisted with running and using until he nearly died from the symptoms his use failed to address, even though he sprained his left foot in a pothole.

For the next 25 years he coped with the consequences of the foot's flatness, minor but debilitating damages to his calves and hams. Consequences included acupuncture, excruciating massages, frustratingly-gentle massages, a torn gastrocnemius, orthotics, quitting jogging, starting jogging, giving up exercising if he couldn't jog, changing to rowing, resuming jogging , hurting his calf again, speculating on whether his foot had widened with age so that his favorite running shoes were causing his calf-problems, learning to stretch, resolving to relax, resolving to do exercises squeezing towels with his toes to strengthen the arch underlying the left side of his basic support and posture.

His career as a sports fan was more spotty: he loved a boxer in his 20s and 30s, a basketball team in his 30s, a runner in his early 40s, and a tennis player in his late

40s. He loved the name but could not remember the looks or the form of one athlete from his 20s: Peaches Bartkowitz, even though she was renowned for wearing frilly underclothes. He hated teams and athletic stars he judged cruel, arrogant, or more than normally self-involved, and he suffered defeat and pessimism when they prevailed. But over the last 40 years, he has probably spent no more than 20 full days being a fan. As he contemplates himself, he feels he can allow himself more time watching sports, and he believes that watching sports will reduce his moral and cultural isolation from other Americans, and might relax him, leading him to find his feelings.

K

He was a saint. He died young, after a wasting illness, but he was not a virgin, and he was neither isolated from mundane affairs nor overtly judgmental of them. His dreams brought him sainthood, his bad dreams. His disciples were few in his lifetime, but they preserved his sayings and his writings, and since his death between the world wars they have swelled to the millions, perhaps outnumbering the victims of the wars and of the ethnic cleansings attending the wars.

His disciples are a hopeless lot, and humorless, which he, unlike many saints, never advocated. He found the hopeless funny, leaving his disciples to intone, "Parodox, Parodox", as they seek to grasp what they affix to him as messages.

His bad dreams were waking dreams, and when his disciples analyze them or him, both vanish like mirages that pull you from the excruciating heat of your desert. You know the pull is a lie, but the sun on your exposed skin and the sand scratching your sweaty body (for you could not resist the temptations to kneel, sit, crawl) drive you towards what you know is emptiness but the squalid brightness and meretricious beauty of your waking dream draws you to hope against hope.

His religion is false, because he never explicated it, never captured its basics in parables or apothegms, nor did he organize or authorize his followers to organize its continuity on earth. The falsity of his religion frees his disciples to worship him in ignorance of his work, to worship themselves for worshiping him—for, many maintain, the nature of his religion is the nature of the human in its sorry historical length and amplitude. There is a permission in that analysis, and few lasting religions outside K's are permissive. Many maintain that his wide following represents the breakdown of traditional disciplines that began with the Renaissance, a breakdown that no religion save his has sought to embody.

To find stern lessons in an existence impervious to stern lessons is a paradox with which his most exalted followers wrestle. The disciples add mere gruel to the canon accreting to his writings and his meagre reported sayings, their work widely-debated in secular academies.

It is the dream of many of his followers to organize, to meet, but they do not know how to recognize, much less address one another.

His intensity on earth waxes as it is dispersed—unlike most compounds.

He was born to the persecuted tribe whose dispersals and aggregations are its history, and whose prophets have been denied sainthood.

Mortifying the flesh and its extrapolations called feelings, transcending the limits of the flesh are staples of religions. K's religion is an unadulterated mortification of the human, which paradoxically lends it its mysterious power to proselytize without organization, its monadic essence communicating itself like an infection.

The power of the powerless, the talent of the unacceptable, the beauty of the ungainly—it has been said only your mother could love a religion like K's, but we have no record of his mother's relations with K. We know that his father was an oppressive, voracious, and inconsistent god, like Jaweh, and that K found inspiration and insight in the enthralling power of random oppressions. We know that his disciples find themselves on a journey whose ephemeral pleasures are more of the head than the body, since mortification obliterates everything in us save a few scamperings of consciousness, but we can hear in these scamperings, if we can see and hear them, the fun K's disciples negate, and a paradox, perhaps not fleeting, we can entertain.

L

for Spencer Holst

L intended to marry his college sweetheart and that didn't work, but after he dropped her she produced their son, who failed to interest him. He became president of his family's company, which went south, his career with it, and his relatives, alleging improprieties, pursued him like balance sheet furies. He tried writing, but failed to keep his children's-books free of his bitterness. He studied the history, ecology, and the political economy of his region as, dependent on the girlfriend who materialized while he was president, he became more and more expert on how the world works.

He damned his lineage and his luck. When he reached 50 he went on a diet and worked out rigorously in Gold's gym. His hair receded but his musculature was that of a college boy. His girlfriend was promoted, and they moved to a suburban house from which she could commute downtown to her actuarial duties. His files of crucial information filled the house, and it became embarrassing to entertain—not a problem because her work busied her so, and because his bitterness increased with his knowledge. He felt himself constantly on the edge of the discovery his mental and physical exercise brought ever nearer.

His relatives believed he was addicted to cocaine. The closer we get by blood or involvement, the less we know L, a principle governing the acuity of L-awareness from relatives to siblings to his mother, who disowned him, and to L himself.

I am his brother; I am struggling with my poverty of emotional insight. But I am a protestant brought up to believe that effort is its own reward, and I am persisting to the brink of putting my brother's case to bed.

In June of 2004 our collective western culture absorbed a shock worse than a body blow. Bob Dylan, whose purity of intentions is a pillar or at least a brick in our cultural edifice, sold out, lending his wrinkled grizzled image to advertisements for underwear covering while uncovering the breasts and pelvises of women young enough to be his grandchildren. My brother believes deeply in Bob Dylan.

Secondly, my wife was a textile designer before computers outsourced her work to themselves, and she designed the tissue paper that nestles against the underwear to which Bob Dylan scandalously lent his haggard visage.

My wife has two pairs of panties from this company, one purple, one emerald. Each sports a small bow in line with her navel. The flesh around her navel is softer and smoother than my dreams of flesh. The panties have remained fresh and shapely since 1993, unlike any other panties in our collection of underwear—I'm certain because I wash them.

My brother works at home, like me. His girlfriend's name, like that of many of her upper-bourgeois protestant coevals, could be a man's name, and it is associated with the finer grades of a precious metal. Bob Dylan is a pseudonym. If you look at the covers of his early legendary acoustic albums, you see the pleasantly hermaphroditic image of Puer, or of a clown.

My wife's name is very feminine, as is its diminutive, and it can be associated with British royalty, with intercessory religious icons, and with a wealthy American colony.

When Woody Guthrie, Bob Dylan's icon, wrote about the famous river he so fluently and movingly sent to "roll on" through our hearts, he was in the pay of Uncle Sam, whose engineers were blasting and scraping to dam that river, inundating lands and caves sacred to the humans closest to native on this continent.

I cannot say that I have made a surplus of overtures to my estranged brother, but I have made all the overtures, and when we are together it is painful, for as he makes his points about political economy, about his luck and his lineage, he hits me on my biceps and triceps with the backs of his fingers.

It is clear to me as I ponder these clues that my brother's crisis, or stasis, stretching back to before the record bull markets we have enjoyed, has to do with his substituting Bob Dylan for his father, confusing Bob Dylan with his brother, putting Bob Dylan between him and his son, between him and his lover.

When I graduated from college, I went to a liberal protestant seminary in New York; I always intended to do good. My use of cocaine back East was minimal and unsatisfactory.

I do my best to forgive my brother for his malevolence towards me, and towards my sisters, mothers, fathers, uncles and cousins. I thank God for inventing secular humanism during the Renaissance and the reformation, for it has freed me to worship the fertile field of my wife's belly—and not the false prophecies of a commercial icon the condemnation of whose repulsive

34

image is inevitable to anyone who beholds it adjacent to the exposed flesh of once-innocent maidens sacrificed to the Moloch of our popular culture.

M

Ms. M loved her first name, despite its traditional protestant origin.

She loved its irreducibility, as she called it: her freedom from nicknames and diminutives based on it. Yes, she had been called reserved, supercilious, formal—and thus Miss Priss, Our Miss Manners, or just Manners—and by her enemies, Man.

When she and her partner "became pregnant" they kept it to themselves how that was effected, despite friends and acquaintances clucking, "Just like Our Miss Priss", assigning her yet again to another century and debasing her social currency.

But M and her partner managed a foundation in the billions. They served on the boards of important endowments, and between them there was no cause in their state sanctioned by anyone save sects wishing to rule the country's crotches to which they did not contribute their expertise, their resources, and their presence.

Never did M or her partner ever aver or assume in any nuance of any assertion or repartee that their union, technically illegal in their state, effused any oddness.

They were hikers, and they walked or bicycled to work in all weathers. Their being with child did not manifest itself until the third month, when a slight alteration in M's tastefully-plain clothing revealed that she was the "we" who carried their firstborn.

M and her partner inflicted social awkwardness: in their presence, gossip—the emollient, the lubricant the luxuriant fruits of society squeeze from and apply to themselves—was denied the visages of conversation They allowed themselves to ask, "How are you", but if your suffering was not an infection or virus, a cellular rampage, a muscular or skeletal infraction, the death of a loved one, they would steer the conversation with polite subtlety to topics not limited to you—or them. They uttered the term "society" regularly, but by it they denoted the entire polis, and they breathed adamantine certainty that society's consciousness, sensitivities and accomplishments were defined by the causes to which they contributed.

Further abrasive was their laughter. M's partner's ranged from a mule-like bellow to a chime-like giggle, and M ranged from a percussive cackle to a whinny fast as automatic gunfire. They covered their mouths and they excused themselves, but they could not prevent their joy from feeling, to the majority of what the press called society, a judgment.

Because M and her partner were present, conspicuously, at all significant social gatherings, you could discuss them only at small discreet affairs. A graduate of the finest ladies' college here, now a society reporter for the state's finest liberal journal, estimated that M and partner were topics at 85% of private parties that mattered. And she confided to me what discomposed her circle the most profoundly, "They're touchers! How can they be such touchers? Good *god* their hands are all over each other. Nothing naughty, but *still*. . . . And they're just as bad with me, and everybody! They squeeze your arm, lean on your shoulder, slam you on the back—lord when she was orating on, oh please, 'social conscience' M put her hand right on an old lady's sternum as she thanked her for her so-called 'great heart.' Jesus, there must have been 20 of us who expected her to honk the old buzzard's wrinkled breast."

The relationship between personality and genetics is mind-numbingly-complex. It is known that addictions run in families, but there is little research on inheritance and sexual proclivity, or on genetics and social eccentricity.

But I have discovered M's secret. She is a lineal descendent of Lambert Strether. She suffers from none of Strether's historian's unwillingness to name the source of his hero's fortune: the finest toilet valves ever invented, valves whose airtight patent holds to this day, protected by a growling pack of intellectual property lawyers M and her partner periodically sic upon boutique producers of the highest-end commodes.

M's partner descends from Henry Ward Beecher, on the sinister side.

Given the origins of their and most other fortunes and fames, it has rarely occurred to M, whose given name is Charity, to take herself seriously—although she can understand and tolerate it when we do.

N

Distinctions get lost immediately we act, which includes react, includes everything, really.

N hated parties, but he was afraid to tell his wife and his son, and despised his fears. He liked, at times of stress loved, to hate himself, and since parties occurred on average 1.5 times per month for the Ns, he had ample party-free stretches to simplify this complex. But he squandered the healing intervals reacting to his wife's annoyance at his spoiling their fun, replying with ineffectual provocation to her complaints that *he* was always sensitive to *her* anxieties.

I have met N many times for drinks, but I haven't encountered him at a party. I think of parties as enjoyable routines—coagulations, blockages, densities disengaged from my mental life, which occurs when I work. I am not a therapist.

Because N could not admit he feared parties, his wife concluded he despised them—morally stressful because she loved them, was eager for more. N Junior enjoyed being called precocious at parties.

Parties are my television. When we'd meet for drinks, I'd tell N to cool it. But that's what I like about N; he's never cool.

"I love my wife. I love my son. They're my whole life. I work hard to provide them everything they need. Work drains me, and I just want to kick back when I'm not working. I deserve that. My wife keeps herself busy all week doing god knows what, and she keeps herself in perfect shape, god knows why, and then she's always doing things for Junior—too much I think—and she wants to *break away into good adult company.* I've seen all the damned adults I need at work: the last thing I want to face during my down time is a party."

The good wine helps me listen to N when he repeats himself like that. I remind myself to order it for my next party, and decide to ignore N's request not to invite them. Mrs. N and Junior are fine company.

But N brings up good questions, and I like good questions: to how many humans can we profitably pay attention in a day? Can we relax when we are paying attention to another human? How much face-time is required for one human to make a meaningful impression upon another? To what extent can we be said to have personalities when we are alone, meditating, contemplating our lives? N Junior makes me ask: is there such a thing as an adult, really? And I wonder if N's lively wife will wear that strapless sheath to my shindig.

N is my friend, and I have resolved not to pluck his ripe wife. But I cannot decide to what extent, if any, our meditations, our resolutions, our personalities really, survive our encounters with other humans.

O

Ordinarily is a bold word, denoting and connoting most of life. If we can find in our experience an order speaking to all men, we are blessed.

I am an alcoholic, which makes me a systematic thinker. The chaos of my inner being, whatever he is, requires I impose strictures.

I banged my head against the living-room wall yesterday at 4:07 PM, denting the sheetrock. My girlfriend walked out, past my bleeding brow, my bloody shirt, and I was free of her to drink until I woke in my blood, urine, and vomit on the couch nearest the dent. An artist down from Vermont was ringing the doorbell. I forgot he was coming. He'd built his own house in the wilderness; he grew his own vegetables; he was thin, wiry, and would sleep with my girlfriend. He was amused by the empty jug at my feet. He showed me the work he'd sold to a publisher of famous cookbooks and to *The New Yorker*.

My girlfriend had a vision of sweat equity. You bought an old house, you restored it, and you and the house were better for it. In my orderly universe this made sense, like the bicycle I bought to save fuel and exercise my quads and my heart. The helmet was hot in the summer heat, and Brooklyn was hillier than I noticed walking or driving. The renovation was an intricate series of boring tasks, and so I hoped to get my girlfriend pregnant so she would stop working with the noxious wood-stripping chemicals, but drunk I was repugnant and sober I was impotent.

I banged my head against the sheetrock with which I had reluctantly replaced the spongy plaster because my girlfriend had been right. In an orderly universe, when you have no answer you begin a new conversation.

She was right that I was doing little work on the house, was getting drunk whenever convenient, was unreliable at parties, falling asleep and peeing on couches, leaving her to take the late subway home.

We retain an inner child that manifests itself when we need it. This summer I was exploring, with the help of a therapist who looked like a rock star, the evolution of my inner order, and it was early in our work. I had agreed that my girlfriend should control the checkbook. She wrote the checks to the therapist.

Inner children are instruments of a sensitivity multiples of grownup sensitivity. When my girlfriend's anger exploded into rage, I was like a seismograph beside an erupting crater. I had hoped she could understand the time it would take for the outrages visited upon my sensitivities by my 4 parents to be assuaged by the therapeutic rock star.

The artist was patient in his work and competent with his hands. He was shorter than I, and sinewy. I was portly from the beer and wine. I told the therapist that I thought of the artist's body as an erection, and his competence as a stone wall. The therapist said, "Wow, let's go with that. Tell me about your associations with erections and stone walls."

Once upon a time I lived in a little house on a small lot in the sand in a small beach town near the Pacific Ocean. In this town there were many vacant lots between the small houses where we boys would play touch or tackle football, and where we would build forts from which we would bomb each other with sticks and rocks and bags of sand that acted like fallout. One day an older boy and I stood behind the forts and threw rocks at each other from what seemed a safe distance. Always in my youth I enjoyed throwing things, and I could skip rocks farther than any of my buddies. I hit the older boy square between the eyes at his hairline, the rock bounced about ten feet in the air, and I was running home barefoot and he was chasing me with a rock in each fist. My house had a wood gate framed by cinderblocks painted green. As the older boy called me names I taunted him from behind the gate, and he launched a rock at me that banged the wood loudly and I scurried inside worried my mother would blame me for that scar in the hardwood.

Sometimes I worried my sense of order rendered me incapable of responding to therapy.

When my girlfriend returned that night, the artist kissed her warmly on each cheek but I can't remember the evening because his being there meant I was free to drink, and free to go to bed by myself without her confronting me about anything. In bed I imagined finding a new girlfriend, before sleeping 12 hours.

The next day was sunny and hot, and my girlfriend and the artist were enjoying coffee. Perspiring, I sipped coffee, imagining it would eliminate the mild vestiges of the hangover the long sleep had attenuated. I did not care that I could not follow their discussion of the current art scene, for I knew that the plastic arts were dominated by money not talent, an absurdity that closed the scene to my logic. I excused myself to return to my research on inner-city language-patterns, a sure-fire source of funding from my liberal school. I was drunk when I made the proposal to the school board, but they thought I was profound. I converted to the school's religion, sensing job security in devotion.

Order dictates logic, or vice-versa, which dictated my plans.

The books on inner-city language took its patterns back to Africa. I had studied linguistics for my masters, but I couldn't remember the phonetic alphabet, so that the music and meaning of the sonic evolution eluded me, as serenity had on my bike.

The artist and my girlfriend went to Manhattan to do the galleries. His younger son had been run over out of his wife's hand, then taken to a hospital in Harlem that neglected him as he lay in the crowded hall with ruptured organs. His death drove them from New York to the Vermont hillside, where she joined a crowd of adult children dealing to the liberal women's college, and began sleeping with an exceptionally hairy and irresponsible man, leaving the artist to the older son, who began designing comics starring Nazis and aerial bombardment. The speech-patterns of the peripheral adult children imitated, inconsistently, those of the inner city. The artist's wife was very beautiful, and I knew no one, including me, who did not want to sleep with her. I was always faithful to my girlfriend because I was unsure I could perform upon anyone else.

But our old house had water-pipes running outside the structural walls through an unheated outbuilding, and in severe cold they could freeze and burst. It was my task to insulate the outbuilding, or the pipes, but I couldn't do it, and I sat with books about inner-city language in my lap, a bottle at my feet, imagining floods running into the remote crawl space full of dust and rat feces. The artist or my brownstone pioneer neighbors could take responsibility for the integrity of the pipes, I could not confront the complexity of the task, the contempt of the bluff locals in the hardware store. And so in orderly fashion I took my biggest rain-coat from the downstairs closet and covered my lap with it. Then I cut my right wrist with a double-edge razor blade, cutting also the fingers with which I sawed at myself, incompetent to the last. The goodly flow made me dizzy, and I folded the coat over my right arm and waited to die.

Men have it easier than women. Barring a stiff wind, they pull it out and let go. Their role in reproduction is limited to putting it in, and then, in 73% of the cases, observing the crescent results with appreciation and pride. They faint in delivery rooms while their mates push and scream.

P would like to do something about these disparities, which the prevalence of prostate cancer only underscores, for its onset is later and its treatment less disfiguring than the equivalent in women's breasts. He wakes up guilty most mornings, amazed at his wife's capacity for pain and inconvenience. He has never hesitated to buy her sanitary napkins.

His wife rarely complains. Her comments on what the media call "women's issues" are even scarcer, focusing on affronts to women's dignity, not their bodies' humiliations. P is grateful to his wife for her mature stoicism, but he proceeds, as I say, with a guilty, tentative quality in his morning overtures to her, a hesitation she adores, for it separates him from the brash obtuseness of his gender. But her loving his hesitancy, which he will not compliment himself by calling humility, fails to eradicate P's inhibitions as he exercises his freedom to micturate and essays consequence-free lovemaking.

But again he is blessed, for his wife loves his inhibitions, the shy awkwardness of his approach to her body.

And so P, whose capacity for original expression is narrow, paused last Sunday at noon, his wife breathing softly and deeply next to him in their moist bed— paused I say after touching his fingertips to his loins and savoring her smell on them, and with joy an idea but not a feeling thought, *Really, P, what's wrong with this picture?* And he recognized, for in this moderately exalted state novel visions entered P, that it was not his fault that his wife's labia, his genitals and (he would soon see in the mirror) his lips were flecked with blood. He recognized with the force of insight that he did not cause the walls of his wife's womb to break down and issue from her as blood.

P's sense of humor, habitually self-directed, empowered him to smile at his confusing himself with God or with the program that dictates evolution. *That's a good one, P,* he thought.

And this Sunday it occurred to him how many of his male friends were gay. He regretted that Hollywood had not as yet given him a clearer picture of how gay men make love; he could not imagine embracing and licking rough hairy skin. He mused on most gay couples saving themselves the pains of reproduction, but then he remembered HIV, and the twinge of guilt impelled him to roll ever so gingerly from the bed, leaving his wife, whose breathing in sleep was so quiet and smooth he wanted to cry, undisturbed.

In the bathroom he peed in the sink, to help the environment by using less water to flush, and to preserve the quiet that would preserve his wife's rest.

American Christians call the AIDS plague a judgment. In Christian usage *judgment* means *condemnation*. It is difficult not to condemn disease.

When R's kidneys began to fail, his already-toxic body became more toxic. His weakness, his pallor, already striking, became more emphatic but left undiminished his defining traits: his stubbornness, his insistence on living in style.

No one has been able to define a good marriage, though writers of all stripes have taken up the challenge. The Christian definition emphasizes sexual faithfulness and child-rearing, even though many prominent Christians who profit from that definition stray with subordinates at their religious complexes, and find that their calling pulls them from their family duties to television studios, theme parks, mammoth parking lots, and political backrooms.

R's partner Q exhibited traits contrasting with R's—informality, easygoing tolerance, a drive to succeed in business. They agreed upon something I'm not comfortable with: they loved the undistinguished dog they let run loose in our neighborhood by the lake. In fact I disapprove. Seattle dogs usurp social conscience and human sympathy. They clog the sidewalks, their owners cooing over their hairy charges in tones I was brought up to reserve for children and refugees. The flesh dogs devour could accomplish many purposes, but today it razes the countryside in Guatemala, where poor farmers driven from their plots by Starbucks send their scraggly cattle ever-farther into the rainforest, slashing and burning to afford their inferior creatures enough sustenance to become dogmeat. Dog lovers are the moral equivalent of SUV owners.

I have a logical mind, and R drives me a little nuts. Here is Q, victim of a corporate downsizing, up at 4:00 AM to punch in as a barista while R is at leisure to treat his doctors' prescriptions and proscriptions cavalierly like menu-items and wine-lists. Why, instead of lounging in sidewalk cafes with the animal, is R not taking the steps which will restore him to the health Q prays for and works for? What's in this for Q? Their sex-life must be gone; the dog cannot be a substitute for the fullness of love with which their partnership began. It cannot.

R coifs his hair; his pressed slacks, his cashmere sweaters and jerseys in subtle hues from the palettes of designers contrast with denim duds of Seattleites, and with his pale gray face.

Q is balding, plump, and favors baggy shorts and sandals. His infectious cheer makes him pleasant to look at when he speaks, but in repose he's nothing special.

It hacks me off that R skips his dialysis sessions, inciting the physical crises that pull Q from work and riddle him with anxiety, until collapse forces R to accept the tubes and needles he had no excuse for neglecting in the first place. But I've never heard Q disparage R's fecklessness.

There's worse: I had expected that R would die, counted on it really; Q would be young enough to find consolation with another man. I notice that in gatherings of gay men, it does not offend Q when his thigh is touched or kisses land on his lips. I withhold judgment, but I can put two and two together.

And so I was dumfounded when Q told me he's giving R one of his kidneys. I mean: why waste 50% of your defenses on a partner whose health will always be dubious? How long will it give them? 5 years, maybe? Q says the doctors tell him that one of his kidneys is doing all the work, and the one he will donate is small and insignificant. He calls it a "loan." He's rationalizing what he must know to be impulsivity.

But I've said nothing negative, not a word. In fact, I make a point of being polite and pleasant with R. I pet the dog, even when he jumps up on me with his big dirty paws. Early one morning three weeks ago I woke up with some sappy rhymes about true love running through my head, and against my better judgment I gave them to Q across the coffee bar. "I knew from the start/ you'd go to my heart," and so forth like a greeting card. The suited men reading sports and business sections thought I was coming on to Q, but I felt better for humbling myself to his foolish intentions.

Today I feel even better. They went to the Bay Area for the double surgery last week, and I just got this email from Q: *Dear I, We are both thrilled with how quickly and how well everything is going. Thanks for all your good wishes and prayers. R is faithfully taking his tackle-box full of pills. We're both recovering as much from being sent home too quickly as from the surgery and the pain. R's recovery is of course slower than mine. We're learning to "give time time", even after a surgery so flawless. His hair has turned grayer, and he looks more distinguished than ever. I knew he was improving when he tried brushing it new ways. Our appetites are weak, perhaps because I'm doing the cooking now. The insurance company is paying for one expensive diet! The only bad part is how much we miss Corky. Please make sure the landlady is giving him his walks. We read your poem to each other before we went into surgery. God bless. Love, Q. PS. We're going to City Hall before we come back!*

We plan to drive down to visit next week in my wife's SUV, which will give us better views of the coast-line than my low-slung sedan, hoping that the warm weather I know to be the result of global warming will persist.

S

for Douglas Woolf

Surely you jest, you jest went dere, your gestes will not live, but they are beau, and the balloon you are riding above the party where everyone in your life gathers gaily into hissing patches of bright faces, round like your balloon, the women's hair pulled back the men's slicked back, you never ever wanted or dreamed of living in Texas, you want to fly from it before it happens to you, before the rounded bellies of the slick men smother you, before they herd you through the wall and into the desert where the serpents hiss too, and the iguanas are harmless like armadillos, but not the scorpions—so what made you think you could just go where you wanted, what?

And it was just as bad inside, just as bad as he'd imagined, exactly as bad would be saying the same thing but giving him his credit for prescience, one of the soft sciences he classed a humanity.

And it was exactly as bad inside his tight belt, the crinkles in his overstarched shirt cutting the tender skin of his hips, the elastic of his old undershorts lax, chafing the smooth flesh of his inner thigh, and he could cry, he wanted to cry in opposition to the requirement he smile, and he was so close to it, he felt the delicious relief of sobs that would send him once and for all, to where, where do crying men go?

Well, once into the backyard when his girl flirted with the English guy, but that time the delicious relief of sobs was a humiliation when the English guy came out for a smoke, and there he was wet-faced, surely you jest but he didn't he couldn't.

The drinks table was, as they say, manned by two men. Drinks tables are more difficult for him than bars—he's not sure he deserved a free drink, and he's not sure if the soft drink he orders will cause a snort, and a snort might drive him to the balcony where his balloon awaits.

The shifting sands of the desert somewhere in Texas cry out to him, though he cannot consider sand without water a complete experience. He might drown, he cannot fry or parch.

The men who manned handed him his diet drink with lemon courteously, a fine moment, did he not need to turn and find someone to convince him he belonged. It would take lots of work to convince him, and he saw no one at the party in a mood to do the work. He hated the mood of the party, the present conditional. He was so clever no one at the party in Texas or any other state except possibly Rhode Island could appreciate his cleverness, and he wondered what country could contain him properly.

The Colombians at the party were there because of an assassination, and he wished he knew who killed who why, and whether the Colombians here were good guys, or just more guys with herds. And why should they be more at ease than he, who'd never fled assassins?

He could imagine dying of hunger because he'd experienced hours, even whole days without food. But he could not imagine dying of thirst because he always drank when he needed to, he could not conceive of living without potable liquids. He knew his diet coke did not satisfy his bodily needs, but it was a symbol.

It was a symbol that dictated he urinate before he could speak to anyone, and so he had a purpose: to find the Men's. He prayed there would be no one there to hand him a towel. He hated the men who stood there in livery in the stink to collect tips. Their smiles were malevolent, they knew he wanted to relieve himself of the party in peace, but he could not because of them and they loved it that he was more miserable than they. You get used to smelling shit, but do you ever get used to thinking shit?

When you go up in a balloon, the gas in the alarmingly-lax rondure—ah, scintillating vocabulary—is lighter than the gas we breathe.

When you climb the lax ropes containing the gassy rondure, you must be prepared for the frustrating laxity.

The round faces faded.

The valet was not prepared to bring him his car at this hour of arrivals, and so he strode across the golf course, seeking alligators.

T

to Rover

Nowhere was it more apparent than his shirt-front: T was a sloppy eater. The most graceful leading man in the Seattle Ballet Company, the finest lyric poet of the Northwest, could not keep food off his face and his clothing. I have never in my 5 decades of work in the arts seen the mundane so threaten the sublime. I would rather be caught in an opium den or beneath the ministrations of a lap-dancer than appear an embarrassing slob at banquets. T has been my most trying, exasperating problem as the PR and fund-raising manager for the merged Seattle Ballet and Seattle Center for the Arts.

The rich demand visitations from the stars in return for their donations. In the arts fundraising rules the politics, and public relations governs stardom. It is customary for leading men and divas to grasp the bejeweled bodies or suffer the clutches of major donors on polished dance floors. It is customary for them to make pretty little inarticulate speeches of thanks in heavy Slavic accents, standing above the banquet for all to adore.

Contemplating T's white ruffles in these situations was a nightmare, for T was blessed with a metabolism whose velocity allowed him to eat copiously of whatever he wanted; his favorites were sauces, gravies, soups, red meats, red wines, anything "decadent and gorgeous".

Worst of all for me was the annual banquet at the

55

lumber heiress's mansion. The lumber heiress funded anything worth funding in Seattle arts, fuelling not only her husband's fame as a developer but also his reputation as a donor to aesthetic causes whose marmoreal locations were adorned with his name. She sat sphinx-like in the background as he basked in his notoriety, and very few of us mendicants of the spirit were privileged to meet her. Her reserve, her dignity, the abrupt simplicities of her conversation allowed or forced her husband and increasingly her precocious son whose mini-projects she backed to speak for her. It was as if she was a female Jove: we all sought her cataclysmic nod.

And the pure pallor of her skin, emerging at the chiseled upper portion of her bust from a gown so tastefully-wrought for the occasion as to be the subject of articles in the dailies and a spread in the good-living monthly, was an alabaster reminding one of classical statuary from which time and weather have removed the paint. The glorious gown was in a cream tone that was richness itself.

She left speechmaking at the annual Banquet of the Arts to her son and to select guests, her central position at the head table on a slightly elevated chair defining her peerless station, from which she made bland but trenchant conversation with her two guests of honor, of whom T was the most prominent on her right.

I ate at what my competitors and I called the table of prostitution, and as I exchanged the expected lies with them about the growth of my endowments tripling the growth of my fixed costs, I hoped they could not notice the fear my practiced mannerisms disguised, but which my occasionally-husky voice and my subsiding into monotones could betray.

I was so right to be afraid.

There was my most prominent client, my star, my fundraising magnet rising above the goddess of Seattle wearing a white tie and white shirt polluted by drippings from each of the five courses preceding the pre-Chateau d'Yquiem palate cleansers. There he was taking bows with fragments of Kobe beef dropping from his front. There he was forgetting his glass of red wine in his hand, and emptying it onto the heiress' right shoulder, from which it ran onto her gown like an opened artery. The collective intake of breath, the little shrieks of dismay, the rush of obsequious guests to minister were suddenly quelled by the hostess's slapping away the hands hovering nearest her and in a voice that slight graceful frame somehow managed to amplify into brazen, raucous tones of unadulterated anger: "TAKE YOURS HANDS OFF! Get AWAY from me! Take your seats! *Please resume, Maestro T.*"

The rest is a blurred nightmare. I remember the utter silence into which T deployed his gracefully-rueful apologies and continued his whimsical remarks about how our hostess had with singular magic converted Seattle's life of the spirit from a swampy fly-blown estuary to a humming electrified metropolis, concluding with mock-heroic couplets on her and her family. And I remember the smirks of my table-mates.

After what I kept saying to myself was the mercy-killing that finally released us from the party, I removed my jacket and tie, dropped my braces, and slumped into my corner of the wide back seat of the limo, refusing to speak as T poured me champagne from the ice bucket.

At home, I burst into tears.

"How can you do this do me? How can you ruin all my work with these revolting displays. Everything was ruined, ruined, because you insist, you the most graceful man on earth, you insist on soiling yourself like an infant in a high chair. This is tragic, tragic."

But he picked me up and carried me from the foyer to the bedroom.

"Hush, hush, my little boy. My little I, you know it's not a tragedy, you know the event was perfect, wonderful, and all those beautiful people are in love with everything you do, as am I."

And as he lowered me gently to our bed I remembered how much strength it takes to be a dancer.

U

I watched two archeologists of the mysterious Maya on the tube last night. The visionary sporting a headband mounted the hill covering a palace to send and receive signals to his cellphone and computer, gaze spanning the rainforest he was "fighting" to preserve. The scholar wearing wire rims puzzled over hieroglyphs adorning a fresco newly-exposed below. Should the second decipher the signs before looters pry them away he might confirm the first's bold hypothesis that mythical kings from the pre-Classic were real, buried in the mound on which he pondered in profile.

I love the little brown Maya people; my heart touched by their victimization and their soulful eyes. Were I not leery of the dangers, the bright colors they weave would lure me to Guatemala.

I sound like a gringo asshole; I am a gringo asshole.

The National Geographic documentary re-enacted the installation of a great pre-Classic ruler. He sat atop a throne atop a ladder, and supporting the ladder spiritually—supporting his installation and the prosperity of his rule—were the bleeding bodies of crucified children.

I am six feet tall, but the Maya could be my spiritual ancestors, smiling in my imagination from the dead landscape I inherit.

The Maya ravaged the hardwoods of their rainforests to cook the limestone that coated their palaces.

My character exists because many people can iden-
tify me.

If the archeologist with wire-rims reads these
words, how will he decode them?

I know what the visionary would do with them.

I am 63 years old. I shall never know what Mayan
calendrics could reveal to me.

Television is universally-desired by developing
societies, but I rarely watch it, although when I am
alone it mitigates my emptiness better than food the
radio or the newspaper.

V

for James Tierney

The building is near Union Station. Good move guys, V thinks, you can get cheap labor here easy. The lobby is dominated by a series of black marble slabs, water dribbling over and bubbling up between them.

The receptionist is a Black woman poured into a skimpy halter and a cowgirl miniskirt, her face a mask of gray-purple makeup, her manner so stylized and self-involved he can't even begin to buddy up to her the way he has to so many girls who've given him tidbits upon entering so many corridors of power. The coffee she implies he'd better drink is putrid, and he's about to ask for the Men's when the receptionist's seeming twin scoops him up and he struggles to match her long strides through a corridor in black and white stripes ending at glass inserted like a flat plug to the hall, giving a stunning view as he nears the end overcoming confusion the stripes running by him and the women instill, suddenly turning right down a corridor he hadn't noticed to the row of executive offices, each of which is plugged by the same giant pane giving on the hectic panorama of Seattle's origin.

He's wondering if he should have gone for the white collar and sharp cuffs with the black pinstripe, when she stops, and he strides past her towards a man he can't see clearly in the glare of his glass, but knows is Victor Vector himself, and V thinks he's got the job if he's already in with the company's driving force.

Vector ignores his outstretched hand, continues typing on his minicomputer, talking softly into a mike attached to his collar. His assistant steps behind his massive black slab-marble desk to untangle the wire from his left cufflink, which flashes in the brightness from the pristine sky and the blue bay.

V strains to hear Vector, groping for tidbits, but the voice is like an indivisible white noise.

The seats are backless black benches, and V takes one uninvited, leaning in to take this guy on.

Vector's preoccupation lasts long enough that V strains to hold his aggressive poise, concentration muddled by his bladder. Vector removes the little mike and still typing murmurs, "Yes?"

"Sir, it's a privilege to meet you. I'm here to help you grow your vital business."

"Yes?"

Vector is fair-skinned, and if he were white would be called a nerd, the kind of ordinary man the technical industries have held up, as in the amorphous persons of Paul Allen and Bill Gates, to be the visual symbols of modern business. But because he is Black, his features grate, do not compose themselves into the routinely undistinguished Americanism on the covers of the business press. When Vector speaks, something happens in his nasal cavity that sounds like an insucking of phlegm, and V can't resist his disgust with a Black nerd with rhinitis.

"I think we can grow this exciting enterprise right into the Fortune 500."

"How?"

"I think China and the Tigers and Europe are great markets for you. I'd avoid the expense of Japan."

"Why?"

"Mr. Vector, those markets are believers in the old US of A. They're huge investors in our debt."

"I know. What does that have to do with growing Vulgate?"

"Sir, you've got to go a. where you're wanted and b. where there's a scarcity of your product."

"Obviously. Proceed."

V knows Vector will not notice his flush and moisture because he's not raised his eyes from his little screen.

"Well, when I take over sales here, I'm going to use my culture and experience to find salesmen from each market to grow your lines."

"That didn't work in Africa."

"Excuse me, but I think Africa and Latin America are not ready for your products."

"Why not?"

"You need to go where there's an established or a newly-growing middle class."

"OK, go on."

Vector continues to type. There is no change in the pace of his fingers. V cannot tell if Vector is recording his ideas, ignoring him, what.

"In Asia I'd raid the computer service sector for talent ready to make the next step."

V is proud of himself for thinking of that one. Vector types on.

"In Europe I'd do what we do in America, raid the big banks—they're great breeders of talent they can't keep."

Wow, he's on a roll. He decides to stop and wait Vector out.

"OK, thanks, we might call you."

"Mr. Vector, I'm eager to work with you. Is there anything else you would like to know about me?"

"No thanks."

"May I plan on calling you next week, Sir."

"Fine. Fine." The "i's" elicit the sounds in Vector's nose.

V turned the wrong way in the hall, but righted himself after emerging into a vast bright amphitheater of sloppily-dressed ugly young people working on black benches at black pods randomly-placed on gray industrial carpet. Their voices were low, and V felt he was passing out of consciousness, but his nervous anger and the pain below sustained him until he found his way past the preoccupied semi-naked receptionist, into the impressive atrium, where he felt that his long experience in business was a sham, he was idiotic to think he could compete in today's market, his shirt chafed his neck, and he hoped his fucking family was grateful to him for exposing himself like this, he'd never do it if it weren't for them.

That night he dreamed he was visiting his mother and stepfather, and he was happy to be home. He walked briskly to his stepfather, whom he hoped was proud of the business career he'd sustained after so many false starts in life. He embraced his stepfather, who submitted to his enfolding arms reluctantly, and at the last instant thwarting their closing with hands to his biceps, and turned from him to something behind V's left shoulder. V turned and saw the parents of a girl he'd dated long ago waving and pointing at V. His stepfather admitted them to the sunroom giving on the bay, where yachts like the one he and V had sailed to Catalina Island maneuvered in a tight race in the brisk breeze.

The parents were followed by the young woman, who was crying, her head drooping abjectly.

"What can we do? What can we do? Look at her cry. She's been weeping and waiting all this time for your son to marry her."

This homecoming was scarcely the redemptive flood of celebration for his promotion at the big bank he dreamed of.

His stepfather asked for an explanation, his mother stationed at the door to the sunroom.

V forced a laugh, and used all his sales skills. "Surely no one believes the offhand remark of a teenager to be a commitment for life, surely you jest."

He thought that was a good one that would carry the day with his stepfather and restore joy to the homecoming because his stepfather was nothing if not sensible. But no his stepfather silently turned his attention from V to the outraged father who was saying, "Why? Why do so many women find him attractive?"

V decided to take a walk, to let them all sort it out. None of the streets connected as he remembered, and the renovations by his schoolboy friends to homes whose outsides and patios he had adopted and counted on during walks when he had to get away expanded them to such vast styles they became part of the road-system, which tunneled under them or elevated itself to ramps around them, affording V no place to walk, and so he went home and looked in the window at the girl, who being still as young as she was 25 years ago appeared very attractive, and he decided to solve his life's problems and please everyone in his home by marrying her, but his best friend intercepted him, his best friend who had always succeeded in business from the time he read V's stepfather's castoff Wall Street Journals as a precocious preteen, and reminded V he was already married and had 5 children. "That's not a good idea, V."

V never knew why he remembered some dreams and forgot others.

W

I pull my undergarments from their nestling-place, handling with aplomb pieces of cloth that billions extract daily from their nightly limpness, each one of us alone with hands, cloth, crotch, buttocks, belly. When my life was in a deadly chaos, I weighed 25 pounds more than I do now, and the shiny vertical lines above my pubic hair are witness. I look at my ass in the full-length mirror, and I'm impressed by its rounded musculature, its smooth whiteness, but disappointed by the fleshy folds where it joins my thighs. I turn my back to the mirror, stretching to look for my scars, but the fatty folds above my pelvis distract me, and I wish that my skin could descend from my chest past my defined ribs to my hips in a smooth muscular sweep, and I decide that the diet I am beginning today will make me an exception rules governing male flesh.

When I was young we tanned ourselves each summer, not as Malcolm X has said, in tribute to the superiority of black skin, but because that was our custom in California, and because we believed a deep tan covered our zits. It bothers me when a woman's face has been roughened by acne, and I am happy to have been born after the demise of smallpox. As I shave my somewhat-pocked face, I try to remember how I got the scar under my prominent chin, I look for signs of drooping flesh below my jaw, and I notice the mottling of my forearms, the age-spots joining the scars from my boils and the stab-wound from my sister's pencil.

The stretch marks are unresponsive, but if my fingers stray lower, the flesh does respond, and I wonder what other men think, what other men feel, when they wash their genitals, when they put them into underwear, when they adjust them to avoid pains caused by the pressure of trousers or thighs.

Dressing is a soliloquy.

I cannot imagine—well, I can because I did it in boarding-school and sleep-away camps—dressing without privacy, something I know billions do not have.

My sister stabbed me because I was taunting her. I was bigger than she, and threats boys from my little world would laugh at dismayed her. Just as my mother could make me cringe by scolding or make me cower by spanking me, I could drive my sister crazy by picking up her chocolate Easter egg and pretending to take a big bite from it, by chuckling over the top half of her bathing suit when she had no breasts, by pinning her arm behind her back in a hammerlock, by firing my cap-gun next to her ear, by threatening to burst into the bathroom when she was on the toilet, by telling her she would get fat and get pimples as she ate her second dessert, by calling her names like dope and dummy, by telling her I heard Mom tell our stepfather she'd been bad so she wasn't getting any Christmas presents, by telling her the bathroom smelled when she'd been in it, by shooting her with rubber-tipped arrows, by blocking the television, by dumping her favorite dolls from her dresser to the floor, by marking up pictures she colored, by telling her how ugly and weak girls are.

The wood pencil broke off on my radius, and I removed the lead tip from my forearm, howling more in outrage than pain. I hit her a roundhouse right to the stomach, and the babysitter attended to her not me as she lay on the carpet gasping, despite the hole in my skin.

X

It wasn't true. None of it.

For it all pointed towards resolution, consonance—endings in 19th-C harmony. A duet, the passionate man's Guarneri aflame above a woman whose small fingers educe enveloping harmonies from a vast piano over whose stippled white ledge she inclines still, as her arms swivel across the keys. Or lo they change places and he crashes and bangs the keys throwing his head back and his body everywhere while she educes crooning and moaning sounds from the violin's lower registers, torso statuesque but her arms furious motion.

In sex, he thrashed above her and raised his body to look down to where they were joined. She held fast to his hips, her tongue resting on her lower lip.

It is not clear what actions constitute drama, less clear whether emotions unexpressed in words can properly be called dramatic. And if drama is enhanced action, what is love?

He walked faster than she, and saw less, but his walking was potentially the interaction of his body with the scenery, unconscious registry of everything like her short fast footfalls that had touched his heart: they were the delicacy he wanted in her, or so he thought ten years ago. Each time he consented to her request to walk with her, he imagined a new start.

But she'd see something for sale, shooting across

the way while he hung back, the interaction of his body and the scene a bitter monologue, for he'd assumed they'd keep walking ad infinitum.

She faulted him as unromantic, a problem in definition, for he could nettle her by reciting Blake and Whitman. Their relationship was a problem in definition: here and there now and then a hip or smile or step emerged from the fuzziness.

He married her not because she asked him but because he knew she'd demand he ask her. The wedding-photos by the mail-order minister were blurry. She demanded also that he enjoy fine houses (they had 5 over a decade) and fine company, and she demanded demonstrations of that enjoyment, as a team demands yells of enthusiasm. He was a WASP, given to gusts of emotion that blew through but not from him. She was a Roman Catholic.

He was given to explaining the derivation and virtue of "clarity", to remembering George Oppen and his lines about it with great emotion—to her impatient puzzlement. She knew what she wanted; she doubted he knew what she wanted, despite his reciting her demands back to her in her own words, complete with time and place.

The walk was almost over; the lake disappeared behind tiny cottages that had housed laborers 80 years ago—she belittled his antiquarianism, and as they approached their cottage he remembered reminding himself to enjoy the scenery, the mansions in the gated community under the second-growth evergreens, the movie star's vertiginous view home, the welcome irregularity of older homes' gardens, the mountains behind the shiny suburb sprung up in 2 decades of cyber-wealth, the occasional sailboat among the powerboats whose fuel consumption he remembered not to lament while they walked, and the turtles and muskrats in nooks along a shore dominated by dogs launching themselves at balls detonated from hand catapults—in his preoccupation with avoiding controversy he'd forgotten to look, and he felt like an asshole taking a walk at her slow pace without deriving visual aliment to make up for aerobic laxity.

As they went their ways inside he remembered how she hated the little she knew of the sixties. Despite being there, he remembered the sixties:

Peter Parker puffed pensively on Harry Harrison's pot pipe. John Johnson said it took him up and down, thrusting his hand out and back from his chest, elbow raised. Harry said it took him down, gently leaving him to climb back up on his own, a delicious sweat-free journey. Peter would arbitrate. He filled his lungs with love. When John said Harry's stuff took him up and down, but illustrated with the flat backhand, Harry's eyes followed John's hand edgily as a cat itching to jump a mouse. He sighed happily as the hand returned. Had he expected it to disappear? Harry Harrison never told. He was part Indian, part Dane. Peter Parker called him the Great American Dane, urging him to hurry up and finish the novel, man.

Peter let out his love with a slow control. Harry had rolled his and John's, but it was just like Peter to pull his from a pipe. John was headed down: he left off scratching his thigh to pick his nose with the hand that had gone in and out.

Harry's eyes wheeled to Peter's; he lifted his eyebrows significantly.

"Well?"

"Well yourself."

Peter eschewed urgency when he stalked his thoughts.

"Well swell." This was John, who seldom sold his paintings.

"Unwell," said Harry.

Peter told of a dilettante who studied bigtime in Germany. The man knew German, French, Latin, Greek and the phonetic alphabet, man. The man was single, lived with his mother, who'd married the young butler. The man was heir to a suntan lotion fortune. That day he would buy shoes, that is today. Four pairs, and not one would hurt his feet, they'd be made of such fucking expensive soft animals. You see he was back from Germany, and all Germans have square feet and shoes to match. The man's feet were ready for American shoes, or English or Italian, they were sinuous again, they'd made it.

"Made what?" John needed to know.

"Made his feet American."

"Why the fuck'd he think that?" Harry liked to argue so you couldn't ask him about his writing.

Because of the women in the revolving door. He was heading into Needless Markup and he saw two women in the triangular chinks of the door—

"They're called slots."

"No, slits."

—They were in the other two chinks and he just dug them there, he just couldn't stand to see the first woman expelled or expulsed from the outer chink and so he put his square shoe between the door and the frame to freeze the women to his vision, but the first

73

woman was in the clear before he put his foot in, and there he was left with one chink-held woman under glass.

John's eyeballs shifted from knee to knee across six knees.

"So what did the dilettante do?"

Leaving his shoe in the chink to hold her there, confident the shoe afforded her a source of oxygen, he snapped her with his state-of-the-art Leica, sampled the perfumes and colognes in the lobby, so thrilled with the freedom to move about an American city in one shoe that he rushed to the taxi stand and went home to his mother.

Harry's eyes rested on Peter's feet.

John itched to know Peter's ruling on the nature and direction of the pot. So did Harry, once again.

"Yeah, come on, man."

Peter held back his fund of feeling, his rising resentment at being bugged, and peeled from the top the proposal that pot is what you put into it, whence its name.

That didn't do it for them. John liked to see all facets of both sides. Harry wanted to make the plunge.

But Peter wasn't done when he concluded. Not by a slung lot. His thoughts were little nibblers, and his head was head cheese, hahahahaha. Crouched behind the munching mice was a Siamese cat, whose eyes were light and dark blue, like Oxford University.

A bell rang, and Peter padded across his pad. It was the mail. It was nothing.

Peter was ready to subscribe to one of two propositions, "So will you please make them?"

74

"Make what?" (John)

Harry proposed that this pot had that faculty of making it and/or you down, and then you had to come back on your own lonesome. "But no sweat, kind of like going to the drive-in, and you idle through the dark to find your spot, and then you figure out how to hook up so you can hear the big image, and the couple in the back seat doesn't even care, man."

John thought it was more like tooling across Kansas, so flat and smooth until an unseen vertical road-ripple gave you that funny feeling like being in a swing when you grew up.

Peter could see it all. "For this one pregnant moment you're both right, wherever you go. It's so great, man, to be right but like how do we like prove it so we can all be happy, cause that's what we want, we just want to go on from here, just go on being so fucking happy just like now, man. It's that innate fucking faculty of assent to the Now."

They stared at Peter. Harry thought he got it, and hated it. "What kind of halfbreed cocksucking answer is that?"

Which is just what Peter was positive he was asking himself earlier, when he got up to do something.

Now he came back with a log. He heard winds behind his head. The fire in the metal stove raged and popped. Then it went cold and Harry blew onto it till he was purple and dizzy. He crashed back into his rocking-chair, which smashed under him. John tried the bellows, which had a hole in it and dusted his face. He missed the farm in the country where he painted. Harry had a house up there too, but a kid fleeing the draft broke in, causing the water pipes to freeze and burst and the whole place looked like an undefrosted fridge.

Harry surfaced. He waved at Peter going by. John was up ahead but they were no more than a quarter of the way up the backside of Mount Equinox, where the nuns lived. It was hot and steep, and rocks and roots protruded all over the trail. And here came that loud fucking bummer of a movie director, the one who mooched all the land from the artist whose son had died. He yakked and yakked while Peter, Harry and John blew and cursed. The bastard had a personal trainer with one name, and he used filtered water. **"Oh, so you know Anne Waldman, Harry. What a beautiful chick. I'd like to ball her seven different ways. I'd like to do it from behind roller-skating down Broadway. Ya know Ted Berrigan?"**

Halfway they rested on a boulder under the hot sun. They hated the heat, but the sun was one with the healthy outdoors. The director was bitching in his safari outfit how hard it is to be a writer in this country, man. Harry was in tears agreeing. Peter wanted to throw him over the cliff, but a nice young nun beckoned him, in her eyes the colorless bliss of the flower child.

But Harry wouldn't stop crying because it was o.k. for a man to cry with his friends. Why was it o.k.? John said it was o.k. this time on this good stuff but he wanted to hurl when his daughter cried.

A noble stag sauntered through Peter's pad, indicating the thicket with his thickset rack, long grasses dripping from his muzzle like Jackson MacLow's beard. They were sitting in directors' chairs, their

76

parents' embarrassing nicknames for them blazoned across the backs. Peter was worried whether he was well-enough read. Their voices sounded harsh, too fucking abrasive to Peter, so he turned up the stereo, "Thus Spake Zarathustra," and it jammed John's ears, and Harry hated people who forced you to dig what they dug, shearing off your inner rhythm.

In techno we speak of *plotting* curves. Authorities on the unknown like scientists and physicians are first person plural, "We treat your symptoms with protocols A and B, and generally we achieve satisfactory results." We fit lines known as curves, even when they are straight, to the data. We are reassured by their stories, our imagined place in the plot's diagram.

We can simulate not only human and animal behavior but also the entire cosmos and its history on powerful computers. Yesterday a scientist called a computer's model of a supernova "a brave calculation".

Fear of the unknown impels us to reason, reasons, reasoning. Hostages with weapons next their skins beg their captors to understand they had nothing to do with what outrages their captors. They quake, vomit, piss and crap, but they go on talking, hoping their words will plot their future.

When I was in college I suffered the math fear that is said to afflict women, and so I took a course on the history of science, rather than a lab course. I learned that the Ptolemaic system explains most everything visible in the visible heavens. But I was impatient with Professor Cohen, because I wanted to know the truth.

We are told it takes a wall to cause a white dwarf to explode. The semiotics of the sentence I just wrote is beyond me.

Few words that have meaning to me, like *feelings*,

serenity, peace, comfort, love, and *meaning* can survive radical analysis.

I experience life as a radical analysis of me. It would be bathetic to compare myself to a hostage, but it would be inaccurate to say that comfort and meaning occur naturally or frequently to me. If you ask me, how are you, you have imposed on me a problem I cannot solve. And you will never stop asking me how are you.

My father would interrupt my boyhood complaints to declare, *There is no such thing as "can't".* Had I the time I would plot my life to test that hypothesis. The X axis would be Failure and the Y axis not Success but Achievement or Completion. And if I could plot a representative sample of my life's discrete events and projects, increased steepness of the curve would represent validation of Dad's dictum. I would need authoritative advice on how to define each term.

Then I might know whether my feelings are true or false.

And we would have a story I could never write, for I can't plan, but which we could all accept, as we watch my scientific and medical advisors project the data and demonstrate their plotting with the red eyes of their laser pointers.

And were they my readers, I would ask them to please excuse my good intentions, which I am unable to veneer. If they cannot, they'll close me and put me down. But they should know that I will feel it when they abandon me.

They can hold me and exclaim over me. They can kiss my outside—even my innards.

It is assumed that I should nourish them, but the neediness that propels my good intentions is voracious.

To be frank as good intentions dictate: my story tells of consistent deprivation. My parents forgot to baptize me, perhaps because my shock of long red hair drove my young mother to faint at the sight of her firstborn.

I look at my birth certificate from the Good Samaritan in Los Angeles, at the prints of my little feet, and I'm overwhelmed by love for all the babies I see in restaurants and parks, babies whose attention I solicit by imitating their little moves with their mouths their toys their little fingers. I know they cannot see me clearly, and they will not remember me.

From the first there were caretakers for me, English, Scotch, and German. One had been my mother's nanny. My mother is alive, the caretakers dead, like my father.

Privation differs from deprivation: I always ate well, too well.

But I was always at a loss.

I was at a loss to tune my feelings to what came at me from my parents, or what didn't. I received plenty of guidance on manners and table manners, which serves me in good stead to this day.

At a loss and awkward. Which led to self-consciousness, shyness, and to loneliness.

I'm not clear on what led to what.

And this is not so much a letter to the world as an intercourse with it, whose pages reek of the games, the songs, the comfortings, the embraces I have wanted. It is my responsibility to tell you who I am as you decide whether to pick me up hold me and take me with you. I would like to believe my failings lovable. In your hands I'm that baby at the next table smearing his face with vegetables.

REALITY STREET titles in print

Poetry series

Kelvin Corcoran: *Lyric Lyric* (1993)
Maggie O'Sullivan: *In the House of the Shaman* (1993)
Fanny Howe: *O'Clock* (1995)
Maggie O'Sullivan (ed.): *Out of Everywhere* (1996)
Cris Cheek/Sianed Jones: *Songs From Navigation* (1997)
Lisa Robertson: *Debbie: An Epic* (1997)
Maurice Scully: *Steps* (1997)
Denise Riley: *Selected Poems* (2000)
Lisa Robertson: *The Weather* (2001)
Robert Sheppard: *The Lores* (2003)
Lawrence Upton *Wire Sculptures* (2003)
Ken Edwards: *eight + six* (2003)
Redell Olsen: *Secure Portable Space* (2004)
Peter Riley: *Excavations* (2004)
Allen Fisher: *Place* (2005)
Tony Baker: *In Transit* (2005)
Jeff Hilson: *stretchers* (2006)
Maurice Scully: *Sonata* (2006)
Maggie O'Sullivan: *Body of Work* (2006)
Sarah Riggs: *chain of minuscule decisions ...* (2007)
Carol Watts: *Wrack* (2007)
Jeff Hilson (ed.): *The Reality Street Book of Sonnets* (2008)
Peter Jaeger: *Rapid Eye Movement* (2009)
Wendy Mulford: *The Land Between* (2009)
Allan K Horwitz/Ken Edwards (ed.): *Botsotso* (2009)
Bill Griffiths: *Collected Earlier Poems* (2010)
Fanny Howe: *Emergence* (2010)
Jim Goar: *Seoul Bus Poems* (2010)
James Davies: *Plants* (2011)
Carol Watts: *Occasionals* (2011)
Paul Brown: *A Cabin in the Mountains* (2012)

Maggie O'Sullivan: *Waterfalls* (2012)
Andrea Brady: *Cut from the Rushes* (2013)
Peter Hughes: Allotment Architecture (2013)
Bill Griffiths: *Collected Poems & Sequences* (2014)
Peter Hughes: *Quite Frankly* (2015)
Emily Critchley (ed.): *Out of Everywhere 2* (2015)

Narrative series

Ken Edwards: *Futures* (1998, reprinted 2010)
John Hall: *Apricot Pages* (2005)
David Miller: *The Dorothy and Benno Stories* (2005)
Douglas Oliver: *Whisper 'Louise'* (2005)
Paul Griffiths: *let me tell you* (2008)
John Gilmore: *Head of a Man* (2011)
Richard Makin: *Dwelling* (2011)
Leopold Haas: *The Raft* (2011)
Johan de Wit: *Gero Nimo* (2011)
David Miller (ed.): *The Alchemist's Mind* (2012)
Sean Pemberton: *White* (2012)
Ken Edwards: *Down With Beauty* (2013)
Philip Terry: *tapestry* (2013)

For updates on titles in print, a listing of out-of-print titles, and to order Reality Street books, please go to www.realitystreet.co.uk. For any other enquiries, email info@realitystreet.co.uk or write to the address on the reverse of the title page.

REALITY STREET depends for its continuing existence on the Reality Street Supporters scheme. For details of how to become a Reality Street Supporter, visit our website at: **www.realitystreet.co.uk/supporter-scheme.php**

Reality Street Supporters who have sponsored this book:

Joanne Ashcroft
Andrew Bailey
Alan Baker
Chris Beckett
Linda Black
John Bloomberg-Rissman
Andrew Brewerton
Jasper Brinton
Manuel Brito
Peter Brown
Clive Bush
Mark Callan
John Cayley
Cris Cheek
Theodoros Chiotis
Claire Crowther
Johan de Wit
David Dowker
Laurie Duggan
Carrie Etter
Gareth Farmer
Michael Finnissy
Allen Fisher/Spanner
Nancy Gaffield
Susan Gevirtz
Jim Goar & Sang-yeon Lee
John Goodby
Paul Griffiths
Chris Gutkind
Charles Hadfield
Catherine Hales
John Hall
Alan Halsey
Robert Hampson
Jeff Hilson
Fanny Howe
Anthony Howell
Peter Hughes
Elizabeth James &
Harry Gilonis
Keith Jebb

Pierre Joris
Linda Kemp
L Kiew
Peter Larkin
Dorothy Lehane
Chris Lord
Ian Mcewen
Ian McMillan
Antony Mair
Michael Mann
Lisa Mansell
Peter Manson
Shelby Matthews
Geraldine Monk
Jeremy Noel-Tod
Francoise Palleau
Gareth Prior
Sean Pryor
Tom Quale
Josh Robinson
Aidan Semmens
Robert Sheppard
Jason Skeet
Zoë Skoulding
Pete Smith & Lyn Richards
Valerie & Geoffrey Soar
Jonathan Spratley
Harriet Tarlo
Andrew Taylor
Philip Terry
Scott Thurston
Keith Tuma
Robert Vas Dias
Juha Virtanen
Sam Ward
Carol Watts
John Welch
Marjorie Welish
John Wilkinson
Barbara Woof
Anonymous x 3

CPSIA information can be obtained
at www.ICGtesting.com
Printed in the USA
FSOW02n0111071015
11871FS